Weekly Reader Books presents

The Horse in Harry's Room

Story and Pictures by SYD HOFF

An EARLY I CAN READ Book

Harper & Row, Publishers
New York, Evanston, and London

This book is a presentation of Weekly Reader Books.
Weekly Reader Books offers book clubs for children from
preschool through junior high school.

· For further information write to:
Weekly Reader Books
1250 Fairwood Ave.
Columbus, Ohio 43216

The Horse in Harry's Room

Copyright © 1970 by Syd Hoff. All rights reserved. Printed in the United States of America.
No part of this book may be used or reproduced in any manner whatsoever without written
permission except in the case of brief quotations embodied in critical articles and reviews.
For information address Harper & Row, Publishers, Inc., 10 East 53rd Street, New York,
N.Y. 10022. Published simultaneously in Canada by Fitzhenry & Whiteside Limited, Toronto.

Standard Book Number 06-022482-7 (Trade Edition)
Standard Book Number 06-022483-5 (Harpercrest Edition)

Library of Congress Catalog Card Number: 71-104753

For Barry Joel, who thinks his grandfather is a horse.

Harry had a horse in his room.

Nobody knew.

5

He could ride him in a circle

without knocking over

the chair or the dresser.

He could jump him over the bed

without hitting his head

on the ceiling.

"Oh, it's great to have a horse,"
said Harry.
"I hope I will always have him.
I hope he will always stay."

His mother looked into Harry's room

to see what he was doing.

She did not see the horse.

His father looked into Harry's room

to see what he was doing.

He did not see the horse.

"Giddyap," they heard him say

when he wanted his horse to go.

"Whoa," they heard him say

when he wanted his horse to stop.

But they did not see

a horse in Harry's room.

"Let's take Harry to the country,"
said Father.

"Let's show him some real horses."

14

Harry did not care if he ever

went to the country.

He had his own horse in his room!

Every night
when Harry went to sleep,
he knew his horse would stay
and watch over him.

16

Every day

when Harry went to school,

he knew his horse would wait

for him to come home.

17

One day the teacher said,

"Let us all tell about something today."

One girl told about a dress

she wore to a party.

One boy told about a glove

he used for baseball.

18

"I have a horse in my room,"
said Harry.

"I can ride him in a circle
without knocking over
the chair or the dresser.
I can jump him over the bed
without hitting my head
on the ceiling."

The children laughed.

"Sometimes thinking about a thing
is the same as having it,"
said the teacher.

It was Sunday.

Harry's mother and father

took him for a drive.

They rode out of the city,

far out into the country.

Harry saw cows and chickens
and green grass.

And he saw HORSES!

"Look at the horses, Harry,"

said Mother.

Harry saw horses running.

Harry saw horses kicking.

Harry saw horses nibbling.

"Horses should always be free
to run and kick and nibble,"
said Father.

28

When they got home,

Harry ran right to his room.

"Horses should always be free

to run and kick and nibble,"

Harry said to his horse.

"If you want to go,

you may go."

Harry's horse looked to the right.

Harry's horse looked to the left.

Then he stayed right where he was.

"Oh, I'm glad," said Harry.

And he knew he would have his horse

as long as he wanted him.